A Beginning-to-Read Book

Away Go the Boats

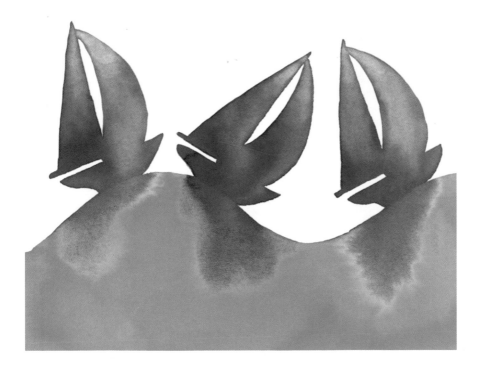

by Margaret Hillert
Illustrated by Robert Masheris

DEAR CAREGIVER,

The *Beginning-to-Read* series is a carefully written collection of classic readers you may remember from your own childhood. Each book features text comprised of common sight words to provide your child ample practice reading the words that appear most frequently in written text. The many additional details in the pictures enhance the story and offer the opportunity for you to help your child expand oral language and develop comprehension.

Begin by reading the story to your child, followed by letting him or her read familiar words and soon your child will be able to read the story independently. At each step of the way, be sure to praise your reader's efforts to build his or her confidence as an independent reader. Discuss the pictures and encourage your child to make connections between the story and his or her own life. At the end of the story, you will find reading activities and a word list that will help your child practice and strengthen beginning reading skills.

Above all, the most important part of the reading experience is to have fun and enjoy it!

Shannon Cannon

Shannon Cannon,
Literacy Consultant

Norwood House Press • P.O. Box 316598 • Chicago, Illinois 60631
For more information about Norwood House Press please visit our website at *www.norwoodhousepress.com* or call 866-565-2900.

LIBRARY OF CONGRESS CATALOGING-IN-PUBLICATION DATA

Hillert, Margaret.
  Away go the boats / Margaret Hillert ; illustrated by Robert Masheris.
    p. cm. — (A Beginning-to-Read book)
    Summary: During her bath a young girl takes an imaginary ocean voyage to a tropical island.
    ISBN-13: 978-1-59953-146-5 (lib. ed. : alk. paper)
    ISBN-10: 1-59953-146-1 (lib. ed. : alk. paper) [1. Baths—Fiction.] I.
  Masheris, Robert, ill. II. Title.
    PZ7.H558Aw 2008
    [E]—dc22   2007046242

Beginning-to-Read series (c) 2009 by Margaret Hillert.
Library edition published by permission of Pearson Education, Inc. in arrangement with Norwood House Press, Inc. All rights reserved.
This book was originally published by Follett Publishing Company in 1981.

Mother said, "Come on now.
I want you to get in here.
Get in. Get in."

The girl said, "Do I have to?
I do not want to.
I want to play."

Mother said, "Yes, yes.
Here is something for
you to play with.
Here is a boat.
A little blue boat."

"Oh, good," said the girl.
"My little blue boat.
I like this boat.
It is fun to play with."

Mother said, "Jump in.
Jump in, and I will go.
I have work to do.
You have work to do, too.
Do it. Do it."

"This is a good, good boat.
Go, boat, go.
Go, go, go."

Now I will play that this boat is a big one.
I will get on it.
I will go away, away.

Here I am on my big boat.
I can make it go
where I want it to go.

Where will I go?
What will I find?
What will I see?

11

Look, look.
I see three boats.
One, two, three boats.
Away go the boats.

And away I go, too.
On and on I go.
What fun!
What fun!

Look up.
Up, up, up.
Way, way up.
Look what I see.

Now look at that.
How big it is.
Big, big, big.
How it can jump!

17

Here is a good spot.
I can get out here.
I can look for something.

19

Oh, who are you?
My, you are a pretty one.
Red and yellow.
Blue and green.

And look here.
Oh, what do I see here?
One, two, three little ones.
Three funny little ones.

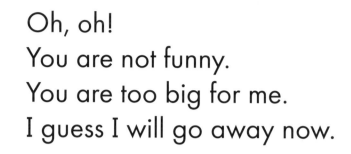

Oh, oh!
You are not funny.
You are too big for me.
I guess I will go away now.

Here I go.
Away, away.
What a good ride this is!

"Oh, Mother.
Do I have to get out now?
I like it here.
It is fun."

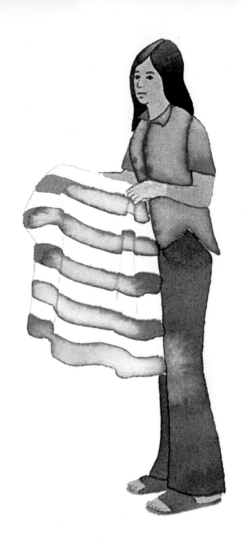

"Yes, yes.
Get out. Get out.
Come out now.
I will help you."

"I will get out, but I will take the boat with me. It is a good little boat."

READING REINFORCEMENT

The following activities support the findings of the National Reading Panel that determined the most effective components for reading instruction are: Phonemic Awareness, Phonics, Vocabulary, Fluency, and Text Comprehension.

Phonemic Awareness: Phonogram -ay

Oral Blending: Say the beginning sounds and word endings below for your child. Ask your child to say the new word made by blending the beginning and ending word parts together:

/b/ + ay = bay	/m/ + ay = may	/tr/ + ay = tray
/r/ + ay = ray	/p/ + ay = pay	/h/ + ay = hay
/w/ + ay = way	/pl/ + ay = play	/s/ + ay = say
/d/ + ay = day	/l/ + ay = lay	/gr/ + ay = gray
/st/ + ay = stay	/cl/ + ay = clay	

Phonics: Phonogram -ay

1. Write the following phonogram (word ending) ten times in a row on a piece of paper: _ay

2. For each row, help your child write a letter (or letters) in the blank to make a word. If you have letter tiles, or magnetic letters, it may help your child to move the letter into the space.

3. Ask your child to read the rhyming words.

Vocabulary: Story-Related Words

1. Write the following words on sticky note paper and point to them as you read them to your child:

   seagulls   dolphins   parrot   monkeys   lion   telescope

2. Mix the words up. Say each word in random order and ask your child to point to the correct word as you say it.

3. Mix the words up and ask your child to read as many as he or she can.

4. Ask your child to place the sticky notes on the correct page for each word that describes something in the story.

5. Say the following sentences aloud and ask your child to point to the word that is described:

- The girl looked through the _____ to see the faraway boats. (telescope)
- She looked up to see the _____ flying above her. (seagulls)
- The _____ jumped out of the water. (dolphins)
- She thought the _____ was pretty. (parrot)
- On the island, she saw _____ climbing in the trees. (monkeys)
- When she saw the _____ she decided it was time to go home. (lion)

Fluency: Echo Reading

1. Reread the story to your child at least two more times while your child tracks the print by running a finger under the words as they are read. Ask your child to read the words he or she knows with you.

2. Reread the story, stopping after each sentence or page to allow your child to read (echo) what you have read. Repeat echo reading and let your child take the lead.

Text Comprehension: Discussion Time

1. Ask your child to retell the sequence of events in the story.

2. To check comprehension, ask your child the following questions:

- Why did the mother want the girl to hurry?
- Did the girl actually ride in a big sailboat?
- What did the girl imagine she saw?
- Use your imagination. If you could sail away in a boat, where would you go?

***Away Go the Boats* uses the 73 words listed below.**
This list can be used to practice reading the words that appear in the text.
You may wish to write the words on index cards and use them to help your
child build automatic word recognition. Regular practice with these words
will enhance your child's fluency in reading connected text.

a	funny	like	red	want
am		little	ride	way
and	get	look		what
are	girl		said	where
at	go	make	see	who
away	good	me	something	will
	green	Mother	spot	with
big	guess	my		work
blue			take	
boat(s)	have	not	that	yellow
but	help	now	the	yes
	here		this	you
can	how	oh	three	
come		on	to	
	I	one(s)	too	
do	in	out	two	
	is			
find	it	play	up	
for		pretty		
fun	jump			

ABOUT THE AUTHOR Margaret Hillert has written over 80 books for
children who are just learning to read. Her books
have been translated into many different languages and over a million children
throughout the world have read her books. She first started writing poetry as
a child and has continued to write for children and adults throughout her life. A
first grade teacher for 34 years, Margaret is now retired from teaching and lives in
Michigan where she likes to write, take walks in the morning, and care for her three cats.

Photograph by Glenna Washburn

ABOUT THE ADVISER Shannon Cannon contributed the activities pages that appear in
this book. Shannon serves as a literacy consultant and provides
staff development to help improve reading instruction. She is a frequent presenter at educational
conferences and workshops. Prior to this she worked as an elementary school teacher and as
president of a curriculum publishing company.